Cactus

a Novella

Praise for *Cactus*

You know when you are driving down the highway, and you look out at the desert, and you're not sure if you are seeing the most beautiful thing you've ever seen, or a horrible accident done by Mother Nature. That is what it is like reading *Cactus*. You aren't sure if something beautiful is happening, or if it is a horrible situation created by the injustice of political and corporate systems, or even Mother Nature. The scenes in *Cactus* feel so personal, you feel like a stalker in the lives of the characters, like you might be intruding. Perkins does what classic literature does. He invites you to witness an accident, and like the desert, it is beautiful.

-Noah Cicero, author of *Nature Documentary*

Cactus centers on one of those edge-of-the-cliff moments when you either take a step back or make the leap to elevate (or fuck) your life completely. Goddamn good.

-Adam Gnade, author of *Locust House*

A good read. Quickly paced. Well-told. Nathaniel Kennon Perkins writes in clear, compelling prose about how we end up in lives we don't want, that choose us as much as we choose them. This is a story about trying to get free. Shades of Updike's "A&P" but much less boring.

-Bart Schaneman, author of *Someplace Else*

Cactus

by Nathaniel Kennon Perkins

Trident Press
Boulder, CO

Copyright © 2018 by Nathaniel Kennon Perkins

This book is a work of fiction. The characters, incidents, and dialogue are drawn from the author's imagination and are not to be construed as real. Any resemblance to actual events or persons, living or dead, is entirely coincidental.

Published by Trident Press
940 Pearl St.
Boulder, CO 80302

ISBN: 978-0-9992499-3-2

Cover painting by Andrew Alba.
IG: @andrew.alba

For all the pups.

I

I sat in the passenger seat of the Chevy work truck, glad for its air conditioning. The sun beat down, and I tried not to space out too hard. I was supposed to be alert at all times. Officer Effinger was at the wheel, chewing tobacco and spitting the stinking brown liquid into a Big Gulp cup. The light shined off his big ugly shaved head. Three hundred sunny days a year, and the ugly gleam of skull and pink flesh was all I got out of that beautiful weather. He drove slowly, less than five miles per hour. The hazard lights flashed and highway traffic zoomed by.

I stared out the window at the prisoners: men in yellow reflective vests and hardhats. They picked up garbage and put it into bright orange plastic bags that they carried. They didn't use the old-fashioned kind of sticks that had a nail on the point, like you see in movies, but the kind with a plastic trigger on the handle that controlled the little grabbing mechanism on the end. The prisoners had been carefully selected for the program—no sex offenders, nobody with a history of violence or a high escape risk—but nails pointing out from the ends of long sticks still seemed too dangerous to give to criminals. For every human, free or imprisoned, me even, the temptation to stab somebody in the neck with something sharp was already very high.

One of the prisoners waved for us to stop. Effinger put on the brakes.

I rolled the window down. The heat came in like a cartoon boxing glove on a spring.

The prisoner who stopped us was Little Guy. Little Guy was in his mid-twenties, Salvadoran, busted a few years ago for possession of meth with intent to distribute. Though he seemed to be mostly reformed, he still had the look of the drug about him, eyes like ice cubes that were beginning to melt and veins that stood out of his neck like bridge cables. He was about five-two and as wiry as an electric guitar sting.

He leaned in the window.

"Hands off the vehicle, inmate," said Effinger. "Fucking asshole."

"What do you have?" I asked.

Little Guy said nothing—he had learned to survive by hardly ever opening his mouth—but he handed me somebody's driver's license that he had found on the ground.

"Great," I said, and I took the card.

"Get back to work," said Effinger.

I raised the window. Effinger spat into the cup. Little Guy went back to picking up trash.

The inmates found all sorts of things by the side of the highway: Hub caps, beer cans, paper bags from Taco Bell, broken cell phones, empty cigarette boxes, newspapers, worn out shoes, milk cartons, magazines, and size double-D bras. Once, one of them found a French horn with the bell smashed flat, like it had been run over by a truck. They stuffed these things into the orange bags, which they then stacked in piles by the side of the road for the D.O.T. guys to come pick up later. Anything of value—credit cards, ID cards, or jewelry, typically—they turned over to us, and we stowed it in a plastic bin between the front seats.

If Effinger liked the look of something, he took it home. The most memorable of these things was a necklace that one of the prisoners had handed over. Diamonds set in white gold. When nobody was looking, Effinger slipped the piece into his lunch box.

He said, "Tonight I'm going to take a picture of my wife wearing nothing but this necklace, and then I'm going to put it on the internet."

He meant the picture, not the necklace.

I thought that sooner or later that necklace would probably end up on the side of a road somewhere again.

Unlike the inmates, Effinger and I weren't subjected to a full pat down at the end of every day. While they were unable to sneak any scavenged contraband back inside the prison, Effinger could basically do whatever he wanted. He knew how to play the game, and everyone was afraid of him. Rage hung about his countenance in a sweaty aura, and I never doubted that the day would come when he snapped completely. I hoped not to be present for the occasion.

He chose the radio stations. We sat in the truck, listening to one talk radio show after another, Effinger muttering and nodding in pissed-off agreement with the hosts' commentaries on immigrants, gays, and everyone else. I said nothing. Every few minutes he moved the truck forward a few feet. I looked out the window, watching.

There were eight prisoners, enough of them that they could probably overpower us or escape if they wanted to, but we knew that they wouldn't. If they had made it all the way to the Roadside Program then they were almost ready to be released anyway. They knew that doing anything stupid wouldn't be worth it. Really, my partner and I were just there to collect the valuable things they found, but we carried guns just in case.

The prisoners shuffled over the dirt and gravel and through the yellow grass and scraggly sagebrush. They knew well that Effinger was too engaged in his hobby of getting mad at the radio to get mad at them. Some of them talked to each other. Some of them kept to themselves. It was hot, horrible work, but they were relaxed. They filled the bags and stacked them in piles. They were happy enough to do it. Anything was better than sitting on their racks or walking in circles around the concrete yard.

When their workday was done, Officer Beaker-Smith drove the Transportation Van out to pick them up. Effinger and I got out of the truck and watched the prisoners line up for Checkout.

II

___

Beaker-Smith stood by the open sliding door. He was a big, sasquatch-like man, hairy and with big hands that had these huge sausage-looking fingers sticking off the ends of them.

"Hey, Stephens," he said.

"Hey, Beaks," I said.

Effinger scowled and muttered something.

"T-G-I-F-F," Beaks said quietly to me. "Thank God it's fucking Friday. I'm going to couch it hard, I tell you what."

"Yeah, man."

He said the same thing every Friday, but he seemed genuine.

The prisoners didn't pick up trash on

Saturday or Sunday, so we got weekends off.

My job during Checkout was to go down the line and match names and faces to what the paper on my clipboard said. Effinger followed, feeling the prisoner's bodies and clothes for whatever might be hidden there. We worked our way from the front of the line to the back so that, once they had been searched, the prisoners could climb into the Transportation Van and wait.

I reached the last name on my list: Marco Ruiz. He was a muscley Mexican dude, a friend of Little Guy. He looked weathered and hardened. Hardcore. He had a tattoo of the Black Flag logo on his face right beneath the left eye, in the spot where other prisoners had teardrop tattoos. I'd been wanting to say something to him about it, ask him which of the band's singers he liked better, but I didn't want to give myself away as a secret punk, somebody who had the life and political experience to really know better than to work as a corrections officer. And anyway, it wasn't like he'd suddenly open up to me. We were on opposite teams. From his perspective, we were natural enemies.

A commotion broke out behind me, distracting me from my thoughts.

Effinger was screaming at Little Guy.

"Did you push me, you worthless sack of shit?"

In a quiet, calm voice Little Guy said, "It was an accident. I tripped—"

"Bullshit. What did you trip over? Huh?" Effinger pointed to the bare patch of dirt on which we all stood. "You trip over your own flapping pussy?"

Lane Casey, who was standing behind little guy in line, sniggered at this. If anyone else had laughed Effinger would have jumped down their throat too, but Casey seemed to get preferential treatment. This was probably because he was also a big white guy with a shaved head. There were no obvious tattoos to prove it, but I was sure he was a Nazi. He hardly ever picked up much trash, and he was always starting shit, especially with the Latinos and blacks. I figured he was probably the one who had tripped Little Guy. I didn't think Casey was a good fit for the Roadside Program, but, as with everything, Effinger had more of a say over that process than I did, so, like Little Guy, I just kept my mouth shut.

Effinger's wrath was focused.

"If you ever dare to fucking touch me again, I swear that I will put you face down in this dirt and fuck you to death in front of God and all of Fremont County. Got it?"

Little Guy nodded.

Effinger said, "What are the rest of you fucking homos looking at? Get in the Transportation Van."

Beaks looked at me and raised his eyebrows.

Effinger and I got back in the truck. He started the engine, and we followed the Transportation Van back to the prison.

III

The homeward commute from the prison to my cramped second-level apartment on the east side of Colorado Springs took about an hour. I hit traffic just outside of town, by the Air Force base. Hundred of duplexes, all of them military housing, were arranged the same way as the prisoners' racks, in rows, tucked in tight, and with nothing pretty anywhere near them.

I thought about my life as I drove, and I felt bewildered. Looking back, it had never occurred to me that I would one day become a corrections officer. For a long time, I thought that anyone who said they knew what they wanted from life was lying. I believed that to have such clarity in a world of infinite possibilities and so few realistic positive outcomes seemed impossible. I was only ever able to focus my thoughts enough to know all the things I didn't want. Because the idea of becoming a corrections officer, a fucking cop, was so far-fetched and ridiculous, it had never ended up on this list of things, thus sneaking up on me without me ever knowing it was coming.

That's how I got trapped.

There were student loans to pay off, and it snuck up on me.

When I got back to my place, I took a cold shower and put on shorts and a t-shirt. I got back into my 2001 Honda Civic and drove downtown.

Tejon Street, the main thoroughfare of downtown Colorado Springs, was busy with people trying to shift into weekend mode as fast as their livers and lungs and libidos would allow. This was the same thing I was doing, basically, although we had different methods. It was depressing. Colorado College students stumbled out of their hotboxed Audis in sweet clouds of Swisher blunt smoke, like Mithra being born out of the rock. They, along with the multitude of youngish urban professionals, were intent on scarfing down Spanish tapas or vegan pizza as quickly as possible so that they could settle into a night of whiskey sours and fondling. Of course, the college professors were already one step ahead, their Subarus parked outside of each other's brick houses in the city's older, more artistic neighborhoods, all of them pretending as hard as they could that they were at a party somewhere on the East Coast. Together, they drank red wine, talked about Democratic presidential hopefuls, and tried to figure out how to cheat on their spouses. The military guys were in the liquor stores, loading up on Jaegermeister. The Mormon Missionaries were still at it, lurking on street corners and trying to convince passersby to take one of the Church's pamphlets about Jesus Christ and His plan for the family. The town's other evangelical conservatives were desperately trying to recall the bible verses their pastors had read to them the previous Sunday, the ones that proved that Mormons weren't actually Christians at all.

Civilization was at its apex, and Colorado Springs was on the outer edge of civilization.

It was the American West on a Friday night.

I was lucky to find a parking spot right in front of Leechburger Records.

The bell on the door dinged as I walked in, but the cashier didn't look up from the battered copy of *Maximum RocknRoll* that she was leafing through. She stood behind the counter, one hip sticking out, holding an e-cigarette to her lips with one hand and reading the magazine with the other. I sighed silently and went to the back of the shop. There were a couple other people in there, nerds like me. We nodded to each other. I worked my way through the stock, walking my fingers over the tops of the record sleeves—punk and hardcore first, then metal, then reggae—looking for something new, an EP I hadn't seen before, maybe. I had spent a lot of time in this record store, but today there wasn't much that interested me: a million Ventures records that all looked and sounded the same, or else stuff I already owned.

I had a lot of records. The front room of my apartment looked about like Leechburger: wall-to-wall shelving lined with that precious, precious vinyl. I really didn't need any more of the stuff, but if I didn't buy something, then I had no reason to stop at the register on my way out. The pretty, punk cashier was at the register. I diddled around for a little bit, sneaking peeks at her. She had long black hair and wore impossibly dark lipstick. Finally, I settled on a beat up, seven-dollar repress of *The World's Greatest Gospel Singer*, by Mahalia Jackson. I didn't care about it too much—gospel music fell somewhere just outside of my usual interests—but it was something, so I picked it up and took it to the register.

I stood, waiting.

She wore thick eyeliner, gold hoop earrings, and a torn up Misfits t-shirt. She still didn't look up.

I cleared my throat.

She kept looking at her magazine.

I waited.

Then, not because I wanted her to, but only because she absolutely felt like it, she carefully put down the magazine and raised her eyes to meet mine. Her gaze had the intensity of photojournalism from a warzone. I blinked and looked away, refocusing my eyes on a spot just over her right shoulder.

"Um," I said.

I put the record on the scratched glass countertop.

"That's all," I said.

She punched something into her computer. The total came up in blocky, bright green letters on the register's display: $7.53.

I swiped my card and put in my pin. I fumbled to get my card back in my wallet. My hands were sweaty. She held out the bag for me, frowning. Finally, I took it.

I said, "Thank you. Have a great day."

She picked up her magazine.

I left the store. The bell on the door

dinged. I got in my car and drove home.
God, she's fucking incredible, I thought.

IV

On Saturday and Sunday, I just sat around looking at the internet and listening to records. I was restless and also completely uninterested by anything, especially because I felt cooped up in my little apartment but couldn't bear to go outside in the heat if I didn't have to. I didn't listen to *The World's Greatest Gospel Singer*, but just let the album sit on the table where I had left it. I felt kooky.

Somehow, I got started thinking about mescaline. I remembered that I had heard some things about the drug from reading books, watching movies, and overhearing conversations between loud coffee shop bros with Hunter S. Thompson-themed tattoos. I did some research online.

These are the things I learned:

Mescaline is a psychedelic alkaloid that occurs naturally in several species of cactus.

Although the alkaloid can easily be extracted from many of these species, it is most commonly extracted from the San Pedro cactus (*Echinopsis pachinoi*), mainly because of the easy commercial accessibility of this particular plant.

The extraction process, if performed in the crudest way, requires no special equipment other than standard kitchen items.

Depending on dosage, a typical mescaline trip can last anywhere from eight to 12 hours.

Mescaline occupies a sort of legal gray area. Except in certain states, where its use is allowed for bona fide religious purposes, mescaline is a Schedule 1 drug, making it illegal to ingest, manufacture, possess, or distribute. However, there is almost no way to enforce this law. In order to get busted for taking mescaline, a cop would basically have to be watching you as you took the drug.

The San Pedro cactus itself is legal to own. It is a common houseplant that can be bought in the garden section of almost every major hardware store. It is not rare to see the cactus planted as a part of corporate landscape designs, like maybe outside the entryway to a mall or along the driveway of a country club. It is such a common plant that most people don't realize that it's anything special. Your grandmother might have it growing in a big ceramic pot in her living room.

(I found a picture of Diego Rivera and Frida Kahlo's house in Mexico City. There were maybe hundreds of six- or eight-foot San Pedro cacti planted around the perimeter of the yard like a fence. I wondered if Diego and Frida had known what the plant was. Surely, they did.)

Most drug tests don't have the capability of detecting mescaline use. Even the most serious tests, the kind that Olympic athletes and new recruits to the FBI have to take, can't detect the drug in urine if even two or three days have passed.

This last fact is what pulled me all the way in.

Because this was Colorado, and cannabis was now available absolutely everywhere, they often administered random drug tests at work. But, as horrible and soul crushing as this was, I was grateful to be employed. God knows the job hadn't come easily. A year or so ago, after a long period of depression and unemployment and accumulating interest on some serious debt, a family friend, my father's college roommate, had pulled some strings to get me the interview. I owed him a lot. Thinking about having to return to the world of food stamps and scrolling through Craigslist gigs gave me a stomachache. This, combined with the fear of humiliating myself in the eyes of my father's friend, had kept me off any and all drugs for the past year.

I'd missed drugs. Emotionally, I mean. Like a close friend that I hadn't seen since high school.

Mescaline, I thought.

I opened a new tab and navigated to

the website of a massive online retailer who sold everything from used textbooks to patio furniture. I typed the words "San Pedro Cactus" into the search bar, which returned dozens of pages of results. Finally I settled on what I wanted and added it to my shopping cart: Two 12-inch long cuttings of the cactus, shipped from Tuscon, Arizona by a vendor who used the screen name xcrystal_cactus_shaman_vibrationsx. I typed in my credit card information and clicked "confirm." Twenty-four dollars, plus shipping.

V

Monday. Work for me, like the prisoners, was the same every single day. They picked up trash, and I watched them do it. We worked our way along some stretch of highway while the rest of the world, driving its pickups and Priuses and 18-wheelers, screamed by at 60 or 70 miles per hour, wondering what it must be like to be one of us.

It was boring, exhausting, frustrating, and meaningless to be us.

To listen to Effinger's hateful talk radio shows.

To be hot and covered in a layer of dust.

To watch the orange plastic bags slowly fill up with God knows what, over and over again, and then build up into a series of lumpy mountains, spaced out down the highway.

To watch the Nazi Lane Casey push Little Guy around while everybody else clenched their teeth and averted their eyes. Except Marco Ruiz, the prisoner with the Black Flag bars on his face. Marco Ruiz didn't look away. Marco Ruiz looked pissed.

We were all being paid what society thought we were worth. The prisoners were paid with hard labor, and I was paid with sub-adequate healthcare and wages just above the state minimum, just enough for rent and payments on my student loans.

The most interesting item anyone picked up with his grabber that day was a desiccated turtle, somebody's dead pet. The leathery creature looked like it had been some sort of water-dwelling species of turtle, but in the dry high mountain desert it was far outside of it's natural habitat. The closest body of water, the Arkansas River, was miles away.

I did my part during Checkout, and as always I ended with Marco Ruiz. I looked at him carefully, then at his picture on the sheet, and then back at him. Each time I looked at his face or his mugshot, he seemed more and more familiar to me. I knew him from somewhere—somewhere other than work—but I couldn't put my finger on where that somewhere was.

When the prisoners were finally all in the Transportation Van, Beaks slid the door shut, and grinned at me.

"How was your weekend, Stephens?"

"Pretty good man. You know, pretty chill."

"Yeah, I hear that."

"What about yours?"

"I've been getting into, like, trying to be more active, you know, get some exercise. Calisthenics and all that."

"You hitting the gym or something?"

"Nah, man. I went bowling."

I laughed and said, "Damn, I haven't bowled in years. Sounds like fun."

"We ought to roll a few balls sometime, Stephens. You know, chill and stuff."

"That sounds like a good time, man. Let's do that."

He nodded, looked at his size-13 boots and then slapped the side of the Transportation Van twice.

"Welp," he said. "See ya."

"See you, homie."

He got in and started the engine.

I walked back to the truck.

Effinger spat in the Big Gulp cup and said, "That's sweet, you know? You and Beaker-Smith got a date all lined up and everything. You'll make a cute couple."

"Thanks, Effinger. That means a lot coming from you." Then, before he could come up with something else clever, I said, "How'd your wife like the diamond necklace?"

"Almost as much as she liked the pearl necklace I gave her right afterwards."

I was sorry I had asked.

VI

It was during the drive back to Colorado Springs, with "Warthog" by the Ramones playing on the stereo, when I realized where it was that I knew Marco Ruiz from.

VII

I squealed the Civic into a spot and ran across the parking lot and up the concrete stairs of my building. At the door of my apartment, I fumbled with the keys, stupidly turning them over in my hands, seemingly unable to get a grip, unable to find the one I needed.

"Jesus Christ, come on," I muttered.

Finally, I got the door open and threw my backpack down on the sofa. I ran to a shelf of records and started scanning through the L's. The Lambrettas, LiLiPUT, nothing that started with the word "Los." But I was sure—no, of course—it was filed under T.

I found it. Right at the beginning of the section.

Los Tarta-tartamudos.

A self-titled seven-inch with eight tracks. The vinyl and the sleeve were both a little battered, worn with a love that I had forgotten until now. What I held in my hands was one of the first records I had ever purchased. I put it on the turntable and dropped the needle. Short, fast, and loud. As the music hit my ears, the memories came back.

VIII

Fourteen years old.

A dork like any young, white kid who had recently figured out how to use Napster well enough to download mp3s of the most aboveground punk imaginable.

I thought I was a punk, but I didn't know what the hell punk was.

But that summer everything changed. My parents flew me out to visit my cousin Jared in Des Moines. The city was not a cultural Mecca by any means, but Jared was a couple years older than I was, and he was the realest punk rocker I had ever met. He had a mohawk and he played in a band.

Every night for two weeks we stayed up late to sneak out of the house so that he could show off all the trouble he knew how to get into. It was a trip of firsts for me. First time drinking booze. First time smoking cigarettes. First time writing graffiti, eating out of a dumpster, seeing actual human breasts (with nipples!) in real life.

Most of these things happened on the same night—a night that centered around the first house show that I ever went to. Jared's band, The Cormacs, was opening the show, so he brought me along. I helped the band move their gear from the practice space where it was set up (in the drummer's parents' basement) into Jared's parents' truck—my Uncle Don and Aunt Liza's Toyota T100—and over to where the show was happening.

The venue was a tiny, pink, cube-shaped place plopped down in the middle of an overgrown lot that had been collecting trash since the 1970s, definitely the dumpiest place on the block. Outside were a bunch of surly punks milling around, and inside were obscene posters on the walls and a pyramid of empty beer cans in a corner. I had never seen anything like it before. I helped the band carry in their instrument and amps. Before long, a small crowd gathered, and the Cormacs started playing. More than I remember what all the music sounded like, I remember how hot the night was, especially because the house had no air conditioning and the doors had to stay shut so that the neighbors wouldn't call in a noise complaint to the police. The energy was electric, and by the time the Cormacs finished their short set, my clothes were drenched with as much of everyone else's sweat as my own. We were animals, apes or eels or something weird. At least that's how I felt that summer when I was 14 years old.

They turned off their amps and the front door swung open, releasing the crowd into the front yard like a wall of water from a broken dam. We flattened the overgrown lawn. Somebody handed me a cigarette. I had never seen anyone with a dreadlock rattail before that moment. It might have been the spliff I had helped smoke before the show, but the experience suddenly seemed overwhelming in its significance.

We all milled around for a while (that's when I saw the boobs), and after a few minutes we went back in for the next band. They were a hardcore group from Cleveland called Los Tarta-tartamu-dos. They were loud and pissed off, and they whipped the crowd into the sort of frenzy that I have never seen at any show since. They sang only in Spanish. To end the set—I think this must have been a political statement, although I couldn't understand exactly what was going on— the singer wrapped the microphone cable around his neck and pulled upward on it until he turned purple and passed out in a heap on the damp floor.

It was terrifying.

It was the best night of my life up to that point.

The singer had a Black Flag face tat-too, right under his left eye.

IX

In my apartment, the A-side of the record ended, bringing me back to reality. I turned the record sleeve over in my hand. The cover art was a poorly Xeroxed image of a crew of Mexican migrant workers riding in the back of a pickup truck. On the back was only text—the track listing and a couple paragraphs in Spanish that I couldn't figure out. I looked inside the sleeve for an insert or something. There was none. No picture of the band anywhere.

X

The bell on the door of Leechburger records dinged, and as usual the cashier didn't look up. I surprised myself by walking right up to the counter and opening my mouth with what I hoped seemed like confidence.

"Hey," I said.

She blinked and looked as shocked as I was. I think she was used to all us record store nerds worshipping her shamefully from afar.

She sort of smiled and nodded, and I plopped my Tarta-tartamudos record down on the counter.

"I'm looking for more albums from these guys? You have any?"

Witnessing her reaction to my question was a spiritual experience that even the Mormons and the Focus on the Family folk couldn't have denied. It was like looking at the blue marble of earth from outer space. It was like seeing an angel hovering in the air above you, standing in a pillar of light and holding a golden book. Her eyes opened wide, and then she smiled.

"Los Tarta-tartamudos," she said, "are my favorite fucking band."

She said her name was Sofia. She leaned forward comfortably on the counter and turned my record over in her hands.

"As far as I know," she said, "They only released two seven-inches, plus a mega rare demo tape." An adorable look of smugness passed briefly over her face. "I own all three, but I've never seen any of that stuff come through here."

I told her that Los Tarta-tartamudos played at the first punk show I'd ever been to and that I had been feeling nostalgic.

I didn't tell her anything else.

"Yeah, I saw them once too," she said. "In Salt Lake City. They blew my mind."

"I was trying to remember what the

members of the band looked like."

"Like fucking badasses, that's what. Their picture is on *Amor y el boxeo*, the record that came out before this one. You could probably look it up on the internet, you know."

"Yeah, I know, but it's not the same."
She nodded.

"Listen, come in tomorrow—no, I don't work tomorrow—come in on Wednesday. I'll bring my collection. I can show you. I think I have a copy of this hardcore zine that has an interview with them too. I'll get all that shit together."

"Amazing," I said.

"What was your name, again?" she asked.

"Will Stephens."

"Nice to meet you, Will." She stuck her hand out and I shook it. "You'll come in Wednesday, right?"

I nodded.

"Wednesday."

XI

For I while I had been feeling that it had become more difficult for me to transition back and forth. It used to be that I could, at least to some extent, exist within a state of extreme cognitive dissonance. I could put on my prison guard uniform, take it off, walk around the city, listen to my records, put on the uniform again, go back to the highway. I was two people. No, I was a shapeshifter, and I didn't let the animal I became bother me—oink, oink—but now, on Tuesday afternoon, as I watched the former lead singer of Los Tarta-tartamudos pick up trash on the side of the 115, the feeling inside my chest was that of two magnets of the same pole repelling from each other.

Of course I had looked up the pictures from Amor y boxeo on the internet, and of course Marco "Cebolla" Ruiz was in them, tattoos all there, his head shaved. In the pictures he looked surprisingly young. He had aged a lot more than I had in the years since we had last been in the same place. The holy anger that he channeled and used in his performances had settled into him permanently. I could read the leftover rage on his face. Added to it were the prison's years. Cebolla's anger had hardened and matured.

Sitting next to me in the truck, Effinger was also angry. I didn't think the emotion was directed at me—I couldn't think of anything specific that I might have done to piss him off—but the waves of energy coming off him were poisonous and blistering, like radiation or mustard gas. He stared straight ahead, his eyes narrow with hate, and he gripped the steering wheel with such force that I thought it would snap apart in his hands. Between his boiling fury and my tense existential anxiety, the silence in the cab of the truck was heavy, like the jittery blanket of quiet that falls over miners who've lit the dynamite's fuse and have been waiting long enough to know that the explosion should have come by now.

I had seen him like this before.

I hoped that this wouldn't be the moment that he snapped.

Undoubtedly, something had happened with his wife.

Effinger had probably spent the previous night in a motel. I tried to imagine him with friends that he could call and ask to stay with. I couldn't.

"You mind if I turn on the radio?" I asked. I was even willing to suffer through conservative talk radio if it meant diffusing what I feared was coming next.

He only glared over at me, annoyed already, as if to say that he dared me to touch the dial. I didn't. I looked out the window at the prisoners. The truck inched forward along the shoulder of the highway. The orange bags filled up and were stacked in piles. I sighed.

I opened my door.

"Just what the fuck are you doing, Stephens?"

"I feel like I'm going crazy in here. I'm going to keep an eye on them from closer up."

I walked around to the bed of the truck, where I picked up one of the trash-grabbers and pulled a garbage bag off the thick roll.

The prisoners were watching me now.

I snapped the bag open, flexed the pincher end on the grabber once, and began to help pick up trash.

They kept their distance and watched me suspiciously. No guard had ever gotten out to pick up trash before.

Effinger hated me right now. Although nothing about what I was doing was against policy—I was still keeping an eye on the prisoners—I'm knew him well enough to be sure that he was pissed about it, but there was nothing he could do. He wouldn't start an argument with me in front of the prisoners. If I visibly questioned his authority, it would weaken him.

I picked up trash, nothing special. I moved as quickly as I could, trying to keep my mind on the work, and sometimes looking up to check on the prisoners. They seemed to be filling their bags a lot more quickly than I was. They had more practice.

I couldn't help but watch Marco "Cebolla" Ruiz. His movements seemed so far removed from the onstage antics I had witnessed so many years before. He didn't speak to the other prisoners. He just moved slowly and deliberately, like he had been born to pick up garbage out here in the West where the states were square. Like the spitting, howling punk rocker was a different person altogether.

God, I wished that I could talk to him, tell him my secret: I knew who he was and we had been on the same team once. But I couldn't do it. I turned my mind back to my work.

Despite the view of the Wet Mountains off to the southwest, the heat made the day ugly. My boots kicked up clouds of dust that turned my sweat into tiny rivers of brown mud. The grass was dry, and a little ways off the road was a patch of cholla that extended for hundreds of feet along the side of the highway. The cholla was the real son-of-a-bitch of the cactus family. Each plant was covered in balls of spikes that seemed to jump out at you as soon as you even considered approaching, sticking into your skin and clothes from six inches or a foot away. They were the kind of plants that Satan's landscape designers planted in the vast and dusty gardens of Hell.

This wasn't to say that the plants weren't beautiful, in a way. Even the gravest violence could be beautiful when seen as fucked up parts of a bigger fucked up whole, a union that seemed quiet and peaceful enough if you zoomed far enough back into the vacuum of space. The cholla's beauty was one you had to embrace and love and find some dark value in if you were to survive in this universe.

The patch of cholla was full of garbage, also beautiful by the same logic. Wind-blown fast food wrappers had hooked to the plants' spikes like Velcro, and the ground in between each of the spiny plants was littered with beer cans thrown out windows by drunk drivers.

"Alright," I said. "Who's going in there?"

The prisoners stopped what they were doing and looked at me and then at each other. No one volunteered.

I didn't need to turn around to know that Effinger was also watching me.

I guess I had to be tough.

"Well?" I said, and looked as much like a prison guard as I could.

Little Guy walked over. He looked at me, and then at the cholla patch. He adjusted his jumpsuit at the crotch, gritted his teeth so that the veins on his neck stood out even more than usual. We all watched him go. He walked slowly, picking his way between the cholla like he was walking through a minefield, burdened by the cumbersome trash bag and awkward grabber, holding his arms above his shoulders and turning sideways to avoid brushing against anything unpleasant.

When he felt he was safe, he dropped the bag to the ground and reached down to pick up a piece of trash. He picked up another. Dropped it into the bag. Another. Dropped it into the bag. He turned to look back at us, and he sort of grinned, as much as I've ever seen a guy like Little Guy grin, anyway. He set the bag down on the ground and gave a sort of little wiggle, like he was dancing, and some of the inmates laughed.

Then, as though he had forgotten that the bag was on the ground at his feet, he stepped backwards onto it and tripped. We watched him fall into the cholla, and we all groaned.

He just lay there, and from where I was I could see a thousand cholla spikes sticking out of his clothes and skin.

By the time I thought of helping him, Lane Casey was already halfway there. He was barreling through the waist-high forest of pain like a child dives into the McDonald's PlayPlace ball pit.

I thought, Fuck, Casey's going to beat the shit out of Little Guy.

So I too ran straight through the cholla, snapping plants off at their bases like an electric weed trimmer, hand on my gun, too full of adrenaline and the dawning realization of the shit-storm I was about to be in to care about the dry spikes penetrating my flesh and coming with me.

By the time I reached them, Casey had hoisted Little Guy to his feet and was brushing him off and smiling.

I whipped around to look at the truck. Effinger stood in the dirt with his right hand hovering over the gun at his side and his left hand shielding his eyes from the sun.

I was full of cholla spikes. I felt like shit.

These weren't at all like the little spikes that came off in your skin when you touched other cacti. Rather, they were huge chunks of the cactus that broke off the plant and stuck to your body.

Casey, Little Guy, and I were all bleeding at least a little bit, but we all knew that there was nothing we could do about it now. We just had to put up with it until the end of the day.

As soon as they got out of the patch, Little Guy and Casey stepped away from each other, thus resuming their former relationship. I walked back toward the truck. None of the prisoners met my eyes. Little Guy and Nazi, also both full of spikes, made no complaint. Effinger seemed to relax by exactly one degree. His right hand was no longer twitching over his weapon but was now clenched into a fist.

I limped over to the truck and called Beaks on the radio, telling him that everything was fine, but that we needed the Transportation Van early today so that a couple of the inmates could get back and receive medical attention. As soon as he could get here.

Everyone sort of stood around, waiting for the Transportation Van, and looking at the blood and the balls of spikes sticking out of the stupid three of us, until Effinger said, "I ain't a fucking teenage babysitter. Get back to picking up trash."

They did, avoiding the cholla patch.

I walked over to the truck. Effinger took his Leatherman off his belt, and handed it over to me so that I could use the pliers to wrench the spikes out of my skin.

I pulled out the biggest ones, and gave the tool back.

"You sure are an idiot," he said, taking enough pleasure in the opportunity to mock me that he temporarily forgot his rage.

I didn't say anything.

"I saw you walk over there, and I thought, 'what the fuck is that dumb motherfucker doing?' Then that little beanboy went in there, and I thought, 'hell yeah, that's what the fucker deserves.' I don't know what Casey was thinking either. They're both as dumb as you, I guess. But when you realized that you were standing in the middle of a cactus patch that was the golden moment. You should have seen the look on your dumbass face."

He made a wide-eyed face and laughed again, "Haw haw haw."

"Look down at yourself," he said.

I was still covered in the papery spikes. They stuck out of my clothes. They stuck out of my skin. Seeing them made me feel suddenly itchy.

"You fucking idiot. Jeeze, boy."

He made the face again.

Then he transitioned back from mean-happy to mean-serious.

"Now get your eyes on the inmates," he said.

I did. They picked up garbage. Some of them smoked cigarettes. Little Guy and Casey maintained their distance, but between each piece of garbage they picked up, they scratched at the spikes in their palms and bare forearms.

I looked down at my own body and tried to pull out one of the barbs. The papery sleeve around the outside of it pulled away, but the point remained in place.

"Quit getting distracted. Pay attention to the inmates. You pissed in this bed, and now you got to sleep in it."

I thought words in my head.

Words like fuck shit cunt motherfuck-er.

Asshole prick.

Dick fuck dammit.

I didn't know at whom I was directing these words, but they were there.

Before long, Beaks came with the Transportation Van. He pulled up behind us, and we stopped and got out.

He looked me over, at my blood and the shit still stuck in my skin and clothes, and said, "What the hell happened?"

"You don't even want to know," I said.

Effinger and I started the Checkout process. We weren't even halfway through the workday yet, but we were checking out already. I knew there would be extra paperwork to fill out when we got back to the office as a result of all of this.

I did the clipboard. Effinger patted everyone down, ran his fingers over the cuffs of their pant legs and their collars, patted their crotches.

He got to Little Guy. Effinger ran his hands over Little Guy's prison uniform sleeves and recoiled.

"Damn it, how am I supposed to search you filthy monkeys when you're all covered in spines."

He bit at his fingertips and went back to patting Little Guy down. Hands down the left leg, the cuff, the right leg, the cuff.

Effinger pulled back again.

For a second, just a second, he seemed unsure.

And then, with as much force as he had in his white supremacist-looking body, he slammed Little Guy into the side of the Transportation Van and held him there.

"Shit," said Beaks.

With his left hand firm around the back of Little Guy's neck and Little Guy's jaw smashed against the metal body of the vehicle, Effinger reached down and plucked something out the inmate's pants cuff and threw it behind him on the ground.

It was an old heroin rig. There was no needle cap protecting the point, which was covered in speckles of rust. The plastic barrel was sun-faded and cracked and sandblasted. I plucked the syringe from the dirt, and held onto it carefully as to not prick myself.

"Forget the fucking cactus spikes. You could have poked me with this, you piece of shit. I could have got Mexican aids, you little junkie bitch."

Despite Effinger's bad breath in his face and the flying globs of frantic spittle in his ear, Little Guy, true to form, kept his mouth shut. As much as he was able to with his head in the position it was in, he looked with wide eyes at Effinger then at me, back at Effinger

Then he looked at Lane Casey.

Effinger threw Little Guy on the ground and put a heavy knee in the in-mate's back.

"What? You not going to say anything, bitch?"

"Maybe it got into the cuff of my pants when I was over there"—he nodded toward the cholla patch—"I didn't know about it, se lo juro."

"Bullshit. I think one of two things were going through your dummard brain. Either you thought that you could sneak this needle back inside and use it to shoot up, or else you thought I'd stab myself and get some disease. That'd be a big old laugh for the scumbags, wouldn't it? Haw haw haw."

"I swear I don't know how it got there."

I thought Little Guy was probably telling the truth. Why would this dude who never causes any trouble, never even talks, this guy who is so close to being out of prison that he's on the road crew, why would that dude pull that kind of shit now? What would his motivation be? A real junkie would know better than to fuck around with such a decrepit, useless needle. And while it was no secret that Effinger was a complete and total dick, I didn't think anybody wanted to kill or hurt him enough to actually risk doing it.

Effinger said, "Stephens, help me teach this cunt a lesson."

I looked at Little Guy face down in the dirt with 200-plus pounds of correctional officer on his spine. I thought of Casey's surprising act of kindness, rushing into the cholla pit to help Little Guy get to his feet. The way Little Guy's glance shifted to the Nazi when he realized the contraband that was being pulled off him.

"Move it, Stephens," he said.

"Listen, Effinger, I think Little Guy is telling the truth. I don't think he did it on purpose."

"You mean to tell me that a syringe just fell into the cuff of his pants."

"No, that's not what I'm saying. I think there's a good chance that some-one"—I took my time—"that someone put it there."

"And who are you saying planted it on him?"

I shifted my eyes toward Casey, trying to be discrete, but subtlety wasn't exactly Effinger's specialty.

Loudly, he said, "Is Casey the one that stabbed me with a needle?"

"Well, no."

Casey smirked.

"You and Little Guy cactus butt-buddies now or something?" Effinger asked me.

I stared at him. He took this as a "no."

"Well then come over here and prove it."

Effinger threw a pair of handcuffs on him, and we hoisted him to his feet. Holding him by the arms, we walked back down the road a way. Effinger was in charge here. From that moment on, I would hold the white-hot guilt of being complicit, but my partner was the one really calling the shots. This wasn't just something I have had to tell myself to get to sleep at night. It was true.

We stopped next to the cholla patch.

"Hold him still, Cactus Boy."

I shook my head.

He leaned in close and said in my ear, his breath hot and in a voice that meant business, "Do it, or those spikes are the least of your fucking problems. Do it."

I put Little Guy in a chokehold, holding him from behind.

Effinger looked around to make sure no cars were coming.

Effinger punched Little Guy in the gut three times. Little Guy's body wanted to double over after each punch, but he strained against the chokehold I had him in, and he remained upright.

Fuck, I thought.

Effinger rubbed his knuckles, and I dropped Little Guy. He fell on the ground wheezing. My partner stood him back up. Little Guy didn't make eye contact with either of us.

"Now YOU tell him," he said to me. "That just as easily could have been you as it was me. Give him a good one, right here." He pointed at Little Guy's chin.

I shook my head.

"You pussy. You garbage boy. Hit him, pussy. Hit him you little momma's boy. You wafer faggot man-thong wearing piece of queef."

The only thing I was ever able to come up with after that, during all the nights I sat around drinking and thinking about it, was that I pictured Effinger's ugly mug when I swung my fist. I hate myself for wondering if my rage came from having my masculinity questioned in such a stupid way. I hit Little Guy in the face as hard as I fucking could.

Little Guy fell back into the cholla patch. He groaned.

"You're a fucking animal, Stephens," Effinger said. Then, to Little Guy, "Any more dope rigs fall into your pants in the last five minutes? Get the fuck up. Let's go."

I turned around to see the entire group of inmates, plus Beaks, staring our direction, shielding their eyes from the sun.

We walked back, the two of us with our arms around Little Guy, keeping him on his feet, but avoiding the balls of cholla spines that were stuck in his bleeding skin, and we finished Checkout. I had gotten used to the inmates avoiding eye contact, but I was surprised when even Beaks wouldn't look at me.

Marco "Cebolla" Ruiz, on the other hand, stared straight at me, not blinking, not taking his eyeballs off me for a second. Effinger would have asked him who the fuck he thought he was mad-dogging, but Cebolla wasn't mad-dogging Effinger. He was mad-dogging me. He had seen everything I'd done, and Effinger had done it too, but Ruiz, Cebolla, the ex-lead singer of Los Tarta-tarta-mudos, recognized that I had known better, that there was a human underneath the cop costume somewhere, but that I had beat the shit out of Little Guy anyway. I didn't need to ask him what the fuck he was looking at.

XII

When I got back to the Springs, a breadbox-sized package was waiting in front of my apartment door. I set it on the kitchen table without opening it and went into the bathroom where I sat on the toilet and spent over two hours meticulously tweezering the cholla spines out of my skin. I got in the shower and leaned my head against the wall, letting the water run over me, disassociating until I realized that the hot water had run out and I was shivering. I wasn't sure how long I had been in there. While drying off, I looked in the mirror. Bad idea. I wound back and punched a jagged hole in the cheap veneer of the bathroom door.

Back in the kitchen, I opened the

package to find two 12-inch cuttings of San Pedro Cactus, Trichocereus pachanoi, packed in newspaper. Looking at them made me nervous, so I made myself a drink, a seven and seven. I gulped it down.

I tore away the newspaper wrapping and stared at the cuttings.

This cactus was entirely different from the species I had just experienced. It looked like a lush green jungle plant compared to the dry and brittle cholla. The spines were tiny little things, like the teeth of a small rodent, but I was extremely careful not to poke myself.

I made another drink. Any time is as good as any other time to do anything. I figured that sometime after the thing was done, or maybe before, the world would end and it wouldn't actually matter what I spent time doing or not doing. Now seemed like as good a time as any to cook up the mescaline.

I set my laptop on the kitchen counter and googled "Trichocereus Pachanoi." The search brought up the Wikipedia entry, a page on Erowid, and the history of my recent purchase. It seemed possible that the NSA would look at my search history and my credit card history, and I might lose my job or be sent to a secret FEMA prison camp somewhere in the desert. I clicked on the Erowid page, which contained the directions to process the plant written by someone named M.J. Shroomer.

I took one a length of cactus out of the box and laid it on a cutting board on my counter. With a big knife, I sliced it like a cucumber, until all I had was a pile of thin, star-shaped pieces. Then I cut those into fourths and put them in my blender. I poured in about the same amount of water and ran it until it became a green frothy paste. I poured this into a pot and put it on the stove. As the stove reached a low heat, the fibrous pulp of the plant rose to the top, looking like the foamy scum that gathers in quiet sections of polluted rivers and streams that run through cities.

"Fuck it," I thought, and I cut up a second length of cactus and gave it the same treatment, adding it to the pot.

I walked to the living room. This was

basically just walking across the same room. The kitchen and the living room were like conjoined twins, just divided by a countertop and the line where carpet gave way to linoleum. I put on a record. *Powerviolence Forever* by the band Fuck On The Beach.

I went back into the kitchen.

The album started out with the sound of waves breaking peacefully against the shore, seabirds singing. From the combination of this sound and the onset of the alcohol's buzz, I started to feel peaceful. But only for a second because the distorted guitars and blastbeats kicked in.

I felt pumped.

I sang along.

Not actually the words, because I couldn't understand them at all. Fuck On The Beach was from Japan. But it didn't matter whether they were from Japan or America or Mars. I had listened to this album hundreds of times, and I still wasn't sure what language their songs were written in.

I just growl-shouted, "Rah rah, rah,

rah-rah-rah rah," with the same vocal intonation as the singer, like a velociraptor.

I slapped myself in the side of the head. It was a hard slap. It hurt.

I slapped myself again.

I poured another drink and sipped it while I stirred the pot of mescaline.

The foam seemed to be slowly re-merging with the liquid. It was the consistency of snot. I looked at the Erowid page. This is what it was supposed to look like. I turned up the stove and let it simmer.

I poured a third drink and lay down on the couch.

The record ended.

I got up to put on another.

Tried not to look at the Tarta-tartamudos seven-inch or the Mahalia Jackson LP sitting on the end table.

Instead chose a record equal in violence to the first.

Dirge by Wormrot, the Singaporean grindcore band.

Got back on the couch.

I did my "Rah rah rahs" and felt fucked

up. I was cheerleading along to the kind of noise that guards used to torture people in Guantanamo.

When I woke up, the sun was down. I walked over to the stove, where the swampy-looking liquid had boiled down into a thick sludge. I checked Erowid. I added more water and let the mix keep boiling. I was making two batches. I thought I might ask Sofia, the record store girl, if she wanted to trip balls.

XIII

I lay in bed in the predawn dark, listening to the alarm on my iPhone, thinking "fuck." I was going to have to go back to work. I was hungover, and I was going to have to drive all the way up to Cañon City where I would see Effinger, Lane Casey, Cebolla, and Little Guy.

The dude whose ass I kicked for no good reason.

Because I had student loans to pay off, and I needed this job to do so.

So I beat a guy up.

I was going to have to go again today. There was no way around it.

I slapped myself in the face and got out of bed. I picked my shirt off the ground and had it halfway buttoned up before I remembered that it was full of cholla spines. I took it off, threw it against the wall, and pulled another one from my dirty clothes hamper. As I walked down to my shitty Honda Civic, I used the palms of my hands to smooth the wrinkles out of my uniform.

I stopped at the 7-Eleven for gasoline and a breakfast of styrofoam cup coffee and a Little Debbie's chocolate pie. The guy at the counter looked at my uniform and then at my face. He was an old white guy, in his 60s probably, with white hair and a bushy, shapeless beard and blurry tattoos up and down both arms.

"I know you," he said.

I looked at him again.

"I don't think so."

"Yeah, from Cañon City. Stephens, right? You were that quiet guard that didn't do shit, right?"

I kept looking at him.

"I saw you around sometimes," he continued. "Was never on the road crew, myself, but I saw you coming and going."

"That was me then, I guess."

"I got out eight months ago."

"Well, I'm just headed up there right now."

He rang up my coffee and my pie.

"Yeah, I guess that's kind of funny," he said. "I always promised myself that if I ran into one of you on the outside I'd kick your teeth in. Thing is, I don't even feel like it now. Maybe because I'm out here, but you're still in there."

XIV

Effinger acted like everything was normal. He was even in a pretty good mood. He grinned and talked about his wife's pussy and listened to hateful, inflammatory talk radio shows.

Little Guy wasn't there. He was spending the day in the medical ward.

Casey did hardly any work but beamed in the same cheery and sinister way Effinger did, like the dying world and all the useless shit in it belonged to him.

Each time Cebolla looked toward the truck, his eyes filled with a loathing that held the color and energy of storm clouds. He snatched stuff off the ground with fury, like a red tailed hawk descending on a prairie dog. At the end of the day, during checkout, he stared straight in my face with the bitterest hatred and said nothing. Not a word. His jaw was clenched and a vein bulged out under his Black Flag face tattoo.

Beaker-Smith nodded curtly to me, looked away, and didn't say anything.

Didn't ask me how my day had gone.

Didn't follow up on the invitation to go bowling.

That was that.

XV

The thought that Sofia was down at Leechburger, actually waiting and maybe even excited for me to show up, sustained me through the long, depressing drive home.

I imagined us doing mescaline together. Lying on the floor of my apartment, giggling, maybe overcome by euphoric drug feelings and taking off our clothes and touching each other's body parts.

She grinned when I walked into the store.

"Hey, Will."

"Hey, Sofia."

She whipped out the black-and-white xeroxed and stapled booklet from under the counter, like she had been staring at the door, waiting for me to come in. It was called *Sin Lengua #6*.

"You found it," I said.

The zine wasn't dedicated exclusively to Cebolla's band or anything. There were a bunch of album reviews, a comic, and even a short piece of ironic Debby Harry fan-fiction, but she flipped past all of that to an interview that the zine's editor had gotten with Los Tarta-tartamudos after a show sometime. There were pictures of the band on stage, Cebolla without his shirt, the iconic tattoo under his eye, snarling. The interview was printed in Spanish.

"Do you speak Spanish?" I asked.

Sofia nodded and started translating as she read.

The interview wasn't very good. It was obvious that whoever had conducted it wasn't an experienced music journalist, but just some punk teenager who had happened to catch the band in a friendly moment after some show. Questions about the best shows of the tour (no mention of Des Moines), their favorite food to eat while they were on the road (burritos), what kind of music they listened to in the van (punk). The zinester's sincerity and excitement was notable, even in written form, even in translation. Also present, like trees are present in the forest, was the feeling that Los Tarta-tartamudos were just getting this sort of attention for the first time, and they didn't quite know what to do with it, although they liked it. They made jokes and strayed from the topics and inserted harshly worded po- litical ideas whenever they had a chance. The Cebolla of then, of 2005, the one that I was meeting through the pages of *Sin Lengua #6*, was very different than the one with whom I was acquainted now. During the time that this interview had been conducted, his band was on tour for the first time, young and full of energy, play- ing shows, doing drugs, getting laid prob- ably, feeling confident about the things they had to say and the way that people would respond to them. I wondered what Cebolla would say if he could read this in- terview with his past self, if he could hear the worship in Sofia's quavering voice as she translated his words to me, his prison guard.

At the end of the interview, the writer had asked if they had anything else they wanted to add. The bassist of the band said something about never giving up on your dreams and fighting your way through all obstacles. The drummer said something about weed and pussy.

Cebolla's parting words, what he really wanted everyone to know were, "Fuck every cop. Every white, mustached asshole that carries a gun and beats up 'criminals' should die. Their blood must run and soak into the soil to pay the price for all those who have been lost at the hands of oppression and injustice. And even that will be the lowest, meagerest price. Fuck cops."

She looked up at me.

She didn't know that I was a corrections officer.

A cop.

I nodded silently, looking, I hoped, like I was thinking about how profound it all was, how impressed I was with the band, but really I was just trying to shake out the image of Cebolla, older now, life fucked in an orange jumpsuit, standing next to the Transportation Van on the side of the highway and staring at me right after I had just beat the shit out of his buddy.

"Thanks for finding that," I said. "That's some pretty wild stuff."

"I'd be happy to make a copy for you, if you want."

"That'd be cool."

"Here," she said. "Let me give you my number. Maybe we can listen to some records sometime. I can bring the zine over, or you could come to my place and pick it up, or something."

That would have been the time to say, "Would you like to experiment with mescaline with me?"

Except I didn't feel like it anymore.

Instead, I smiled the sort of smile that is actually just the joyless pulling of the mouth tight into a horizontal line, and I

took her number. I told her I had somewhere to be and that she would definitely
hear from me.

XVI

It seems rare that a person would want to hear about someone else's drug trip. Descriptions of visuals and spiritual realizations that seem profound to the tripper always bore the listener, like listening to somebody talk about a dream they had the night before.

But that's too damn bad.

That weekend, I swallowed both doses of mescaline.

After choking down the green potion, which tasted like the bitterest mix of bile and soap and country gravy, like I had just done the cactus an oral favor, I sat on the floor of the kitchen, feeling sick. When finally I vomited, I felt like my spine stretched out to be about 12 feet long.

I don't know how much time passed, but I went outside into the courtyard of the complex, and I looked at the fucked up lawn, spotted yellow and one-quarter dead from dog shit and the dry air. There were traffic sounds. The blades of grass were still wet from the sprinklers. It felt like the first time I put on new glasses when I was a kid, the moment that I first realized that trees had individual leaves on them. There was nothing in my brain to filter out seemingly insignificant details. When I touched my fingertips to the ground, I realized that I was touching the whole world. I know what that sounds like, but I was touching China and the mountains and the South Pole and the bottom of the ocean.

I looked at the sky and thought about dying.

I thought about the feeling of being in some beautiful natural place where there are a bunch of trees and no other humans, like the middle of Alaska or somewhere. To me, the awe that the beauty of a place like that inspires always drifts away, replaced by the encroaching concepts of property and capitalism and real estate, and I have no choice but to drift into a fantasy of living in that place, of buying a plot of land maybe, building a cabin, never seeing anyone ever again, but then I remember that by doing that I would be destroying exactly what makes me love the place, the land's independence from meddling humans, an unbroken ridge of trees, wildflowers that haven't been stomped down. To move there would be to undo everything. This is the saddest realization in the crumbling world.

I thought that dying is like being able to move to such a place without ruining it.

I was going to die, I realized, and when I did I would become part of the earth.

The earth was going to die, probably sooner than later, and then we would become part of the universe.

Maybe the universe would die.

I wasn't sure.

I felt no anxiety. I didn't think about my student loans.

I went back inside.

I wasn't sure I remembered how to put on a record, but I figured it out.

I found myself listening to Los Tarta-tartamudos, thinking about how much Sofia loved them.

It actually wasn't a great record, pretty sloppy really, but they had created it.

They had put it out there.

The record existed in the physical world.

Then it was over.

I put the Mahalia Jackson record down right on top of it and dropped the needle. The song "I'm Gonna Live the Life I Sing about in My Song" played.

I'm gonna live the life I sing about in my song.

I'm gonna stand for the right, always shun the wrong.

If I'm in a crowd, if I'm alone, on the streets or in my home

I'm gonna live the life I sing about in my song.

I thought about the songs I had been singing.

About the other day when I had

brewed up the mescaline tea.

About Fuck On The Beach and Worm-rot.

About growling along to the songs without knowing the actual words, just going "rah rah rah rah," and I wondered what it would look like to live the life I sang about in my songs.

For the rest of the trip I saw ugly faces on everything.

I ate a Little Debbie's chocolate pie, and it tasted like shit.

Everything looked like it was two-dimensional, like the flat backgrounds in Super Mario World.

I could never make up my mind whether I felt hot or cold.

I saw the shape of the universe:
Donut.

Mescaline told me that everything would be okay in the donut-shaped universe.

XVII

"Work" as a concept didn't seem so bad the next day. I woke early, without feeling begrudging, and I drove to the prison, stopping on the way to get some coffee and a Little Debbie's chocolate pie. Effinger was in a bad mood, but that was okay. I felt boosted emotionally from the mescaline. It was all okay. Effinger and I would die someday, and then he wouldn't have to ever be in a bad mood again, and I wouldn't have to listen to his bullshit anymore. So whatever happened now was fine for now.

I thought, "fuck it" and sighed happily.

The prisoners picked up garbage, and I watched them half-assedly.

I noticed, maybe an hour or two into

the day, that something was wrong with Lane Casey. He skulked and moved slowly, hardly doing anything.

I rolled down the window.

"Pick up the pace, Casey," I shouted.

He looked up at me and both his eyes were blacked and his nose was broken. He said nothing, but looked back at the ground and began slowly picking up trash. He was a sad Nazi. I giggled to myself.

The day passed slowly.

I didn't care.

Everybody hated me.

I couldn't give a shit.

The insidious companies that joyfully held the student loans that loomed over everyone, the firms that occupied my mind constantly on a normal day, were off somewhere, probably plotting more of what economists call "rent-seeking behavior," ruining the economy and making people miserable.

Fine. They could fuck themselves.

The day ended. Beaker-Smith came with the Transportation Van. Effinger and I did Check Out.

Cebolla glared at me. Little Guy looked littler than ever, tighter, meaner. The bruises on Casey's face made him look less sad and mean again, too.

About ten seconds before it happened, I knew it was going to happen. Mescaline had given me the ability to read minds.

XVIII

Little guy had a gun.

He must have found it on the ground and picked it up, like Casey had previously done with the syringe. He didn't make a speech or do anything dramatic. He just pulled out the gun and shot Casey four times. Before he could fire off a fifth, there was another report and Little Guy collapsed on the ground, presumably dead. He wasn't moving.

As a reflex, the other prisoners had dropped to the ground and put their hands over their heads. They looked up cautiously now that the firing had stopped.

Beaker-Smith stood, holding his gun. Beaks had killed Little Guy.

Casey lay on the ground, moaning quietly and bleeding heavily.

Effinger had his gun out now.

"Stand up," he said to everyone.

The prisoners rose to their feet.

"Call for an ambulance," Effinger said to me without taking his eyes off the prisoners.

But I didn't move. I saw Cebolla looking at Little Guy's body and at his gun, lying on the ground. Effinger saw this too.

"Don't fucking move," he said.

I was reading Cebolla's mind. He wanted to shoot Effinger, Beaker-Smith and me. He was worried, but he was thinking, "Fuck it."

He stooped to pick up the gun.

Effinger was going to shoot him.

I leapt like bodyguards do in movies.

Effinger squeezed the trigger.

I felt a hot sting on the side of my face, and I crashed to the ground. Everybody seemed suddenly and weirdly chill, and Beaker-Smith snatched up Little Guy's gun.

Two ambulances came.

XIX

The next day, back in the safety of my own home, I googled "Bullet wound not that bad." Nothing very interesting came up.

I was on paid leave, but under internal investigation.

I had a bandage on the left side of my face. Effinger's bullet had just grazed my cheek. It didn't even chip my teeth. The projectile would have missed Cebolla anyway—it turned out that Effinger wasn't a very good shot—but I was still dumb enough to jump in front of it.

I hadn't stopped anything.

I would have a little scar that I would have to be careful of when I shaved.

The most serious negative effect of

being shot was that I had seemingly lost the ability that mescaline had given me to read minds. I wondered if the gift would come back with time, but, over the next days, as I lied around the house watching TV, my senses never seemed to focus into anything more than a dull, staticky buzz. I thought about calling Sofia, but I didn't. Instead, I ate Little Debbie's chocolate pies, and I watched shows about superheroes, detectives, ghosts, motorcycle gangs, Vikings, advertising executives, drug dealers, cowboys, con artists, zombies, naked princesses with dragons, and a million other characters that all seemed to be living their own life at a level approaching what seemed like its full potential, having struggles and adventures and sometimes getting laid. Somewhere toward the beginning of each character's journey, something motivated them, got them off their asses, and pushed them out into the world. And here I was: 28 years old, well into the story, having barely avoided its premature end, in fact. And I watched these shows and still sat on my ass and did nothing.

The morning of the third day, I got a phone call telling me that Casey had died in his hospital bed.

I tried to be respectful of the dead, or something, but I could only think of the words, "the only good Nazi" while envisioning an image of his headstone—no flowers, just cholla branches laid across the fresh dirt of his grave.

I had a doctor's appointment the next morning and returned home with a clean bill of heath. I would have to go back to work the next day, attend the disciplinary hearings in which the warden and the prison's other corporate executives would determine whether or not I should be fired.

I couldn't sleep that night, thinking about what I had to do versus what I wanted to do.

I got up before the sun came up and put on my uniform.

It was dawn in the shitty part of town, where the cheap motels have beautiful, complex neon signs and racist names like the Chief Motel or the Cherokee Motel. Few people were on the streets at this

time of morning, only those who looked
as though they had slept there.

Instead of stopping at the usu-
al 7-Eleven, I drove a little ways further
down the road to another gas station in an
attempt to change up the routine a little.
But I drove past another gas station, and
another, and then I was driving past the
Air Force base, not having had any coffee at all. The sun hit the red rocks and
sagebrush in the canyon, and then I was
at the junction of the 115 and I-50, thinking "goddamn, I need some coffee if I'm
going to go through with this," and then
thinking that I didn't need to go through
with anything. So, instead of turning west
on I-50, toward Cañon City, I took a left
and went east, back down toward Pueblo
and the I-25.

XX

By the time I stopped for coffee in Trinidad, in the hills near the New Mexico state line, I was well on my way to Santa Fe, a place I had always meant to make time to check out. I sat on the hood of my car and drank the coffee. It tasted like a mix of used cooking oil and sand, but I didn't mind. The sun was out, and the town was pretty, and I couldn't believe that I didn't even feel sad about leaving my record collection behind. I was leaving it forever, just like I was leaving my job forever and my apartment forever and my chances with Sofia forever. Skipping out on my apartment contract and my loan payments would do something to my credit score probably, but maybe I'd just go all the way south and across the border to Juarez, get a cheap apartment there and drink coffee in a plaza, or something.

It didn't matter at all.

I spilled some of the coffee on my uniform shirt and stared at the stain soaking into the fabric and remembered what I looked like. I undid the buttons, stripped down to my undershirt, and walked around to the backside of the gas station to throw the garment in the dumpster. There were two people standing inside of it, smiling and laughing and rooting around in the trash, both of them wearing leather boots and denim vests adorned with studs and patches. A square of greasy cardboard on the ground next to their dirty backpacks had the words "Hungry, Broke, Travelin'" sharpied onto it.

I wanted to be friends with them.

I wanted to be them.

I said, "Find anything good in there?" and they jumped upright. They relaxed when they saw I was smiling.

A girl with a shaved head tossed me an unopened bag of Takis, in a gesture of friendship.

"Thanks," I said.

"Plenty for everyone," she said.

But then she looked at me funny.

Her eyes dropped to the balled up uniform shirt in my hand and then to the gun and taser on my belt, and she frowned.

She and her partner exchanged looks.

"Hey," she said. "What are you, a fucking cop?"

"Not anymore."

"Fuck you," she said.

"I quit my job. I'm not a cop."

"Get the fuck out of here. Pig. Bastard." She spit on the ground. I walked back around to the front of the gas station and got in my shitty Honda Civic. I drank my coffee and ate the Takis from the dumpster.

Nathaniel Kennon Perkins lives in Boulder, CO, where he works as a bookseller and publisher. His creative work has appeared in *Triquarterly*, *Noncanon Press*, *Keep This Bag Away From Children*, *Decomp*, *Pithead Chapel*, *Timber Journal*, and others. He has written for *SLUG Magazine*, the *Tico Times*, and the *Mormon Worker*. Pest House published his chapbook, *Acknowledgement* (2014), and he is the recipient of the *High Country News*'s 2014 Bell Prize. He is the author of the ongoing literary zine series, *Ultimate Gospel*.

Other Fine Titles from Trident Press:

———

Blood-Soaked Buddha/Hard Earth Pascal
by Noah Cicero

"Far too many books about Buddhism get bogged down in scholarly doublespeak. Others are full of far-fetched fantasies. Noah's book isn't like that. It's a real book for real people.
   Brad Warner, author of Hardcore Zen

it gets cold
by j.avery

it gets cold demands a body that is both the haunting and the house, a queerness that is both living and dying. What can be gained by inhabiting this liminal space? What can the inhabitation of dying bring to the living? What can be done when it gets cold?

Major Diamonds Nights & Knives
by Katie Foster

MDNK is a poetry project modeled after a deck of cards. While writing this poem, Katie Foster felt possessed by a spirit who died in childbirth. She tried to tell her story as best she could.

www.ingramcontent.com/pod-product-compliance
Lightning Source LLC
Chambersburg PA
CBHW070315120726
47910CB00007B/2488